Gullpower

Gullpower

Joan Woodruff

Matador
9 Priory Business Park,
Wistow Road, Kibworth Beauchamp,
Leicestershire. LE8 0RX
Tel: 0116 279 2299
Email: books@troubador.co.uk
Web: www.troubador.co.uk/matador
Twitter: @matadorbooks

ISBN 978 1803130 323

British Library Cataloguing in Publication Data.
A catalogue record for this book is available from the British Library.

Printed and bound in Great Britain by 4edge Limited
Typeset in 14pt Baskerville by Troubador Publishing Ltd, Leicester, UK

Matador is an imprint of Troubador Publishing Ltd

For my family,
and everyone else who cares about our planet

Chapter One

My favourite food is mouse with chips. My favourite game is Grab the Ice Cream. My name's Poppy, and my very best friends are Elliott, Dylan and Amber. We were born at the same time in nests on rocks by an old lighthouse, and we've played together ever since we hatched. We call ourselves the Grabbos – because we all love to grab food from humans on the beach.

I have another good friend, a human child. You might think that's weird, but she's really kind to me. I'm not sure what her name is. Her mum calls her Darling, and her dad calls her Pickle. I call her Red Top, because that's what she usually wears. She and her family come to the beach every day, and sometimes she shares her food with me. She's given me cake, chips and sandwiches. I'm hoping for a mouse one day, but no luck so far!

Right now, I'm flying over the sea. In the distance I spot a beautiful bird, bobbing up and down on the choppy water. I recognise her – it's my friend Gloria. She's a herring gull like me, but older. She has a perfectly round head and pure white feathers that glisten when the sun shines on her. There's a tiny black mark just above her beak that makes her stand out from the other gulls. I'd love to have a mark like that!

There's a lot of rubbish floating on the water today, even more than usual. I can see plastic bags and bottles being carried along with the tide. I wonder where they all come from. They don't belong here.

Gloria looks happy. She dips her shiny yellow beak into the water, which looks refreshingly cold. I swoop down towards her. Spray from the waves rises up and lands on my beak. The salty taste makes me feel hungry.

"Hi, Poppy! Do you fancy surfing with me?" And she hops onto a piece of driftwood.

"No thanks," I say. "I'm hungry. I'm going to play Grab the Ice Cream when the humans go down to the seafront."

I fly towards the beach. The sky is blue and there's not a cloud to be seen. There are loads of children to chase, and so much food! The first Grabbo I see is Elliott, dive-bombing as usual. He's the fastest. He's joined a marathon flying club and does races every week. And there's Dylan, tucking into some chips that have spilled onto the sand. He likes to keep the beach tidy. I can see Amber too. She's the smallest – even though she really loves her food.

Amber dives for a choc-ice. She swoops down to snatch it and nearly collides with two skateboarders. They lose their balance and go crashing into an old lady sitting on a bench. She's just started to squirt ketchup onto her chips, but it goes all over her face instead. It makes her look as if she's got a bright red moustache!

"Ha ha! Better luck next time," I call out.

"I did get the choc-ice," Amber shouts back. Her beak is covered in chocolate.

"Let's all fly to the park," suggests Elliott. "There's a summer fair and there'll be plenty of burgers and sausages for us to grab."

"Great idea. I'm coming," says Dylan.

Amber and I decide to stay on the beach. "Make sure you keep an eye out for the crows," I warn them. "They're nervous birds, but it's best to be extra-careful, especially if there are a lot of them."

"Well, Charley's a friendly crow," replies Elliott. "I like her – she's quite funny. Caw! Caw! Caw!" He does a hilarious impression of Charley which makes us all laugh. "And Colin, the one with the unusual beak, is OK. But we'll have to watch out for Cassius."

"Yes, he's really mean," adds Dylan. "You know how much the crows love bits of plastic? They think it's treasure because it's shiny. I found some plastic rubbish on the beach the other day, and I thought I'd tidy up a bit. Then I saw Cassius and his gang glaring at me. It was scary!"

Elliott and Dylan fly off. Then I spot my little girl on the beach. She's wearing her favourite red top, and she's got an ice cream with two chocolate flakes in it.

"Wahoo!" I yell. I'm sure she won't mind sharing it with me, so I dive down and help myself to a beak-full.

Her father is furious. "Go away!" he yells, swiping at me with a towel.

Red Top is crying her eyes out. I feel bad. I didn't mean to upset her, so I decide to return the tasty treat.

I let the strawberry snowball fall from my beak, and it lands on her ear. But that makes her scream even louder.

"My friend took my ice cream!" she cries. I feel so sad that I fly off out to sea.

Chapter Two

I can feel the cold spray of the seawater on my feathers. I'm still sad about making Red Top cry, so I play for a while to cheer myself up. As I'm weaving in and out of the waves, I hear Gloria shouting out.

"Help! Help! Get this thing off me!"

What I see is horrible. Gloria's beautiful head and neck are trapped in a piece of rubbish. It's made of plastic and is a strange shape, with several big holes in it. Her neck is wedged tightly in one of the holes. She's squawking loudly and thrashing about.

"I ducked under the water, and this horrible THING wrapped itself round me!"

"Stay still," I tell her. "I'll peck you free." But it's no use. The plastic is too hard to bite through. "My beak's getting really sore," I say. "We need to get help."

I nudge her head gently and help her towards the beach, where I can see the other three Grabbos playing.

"Help! Over here!" I shout. Elliott, Dylan and Amber hurry down to the water's edge.

"Oh no! How are we going to get that off?" Dylan cries out.

Gloria looks so sad, and a solitary tear trickles out of one eye. My heart is breaking. I must try as hard as I can to help her.

"Maybe we can do it if we all pull together," I say. "Amber, you're the smallest. Stand on Elliott's back so you can reach the top of it. Dylan and I will tug at the bottom."

"Thank you so much," says Gloria quietly. "I'll keep as still as I can."

We all get to work.

"Ouch! You're standing with one foot over my eye and I can't see what I'm doing!" complains Elliott.

"Sorry, I'll turn round," replies Amber. But she loses her balance and topples into the water.

This is no good. Poor Gloria lets out a loud squawk. Her whole body shakes, and she sobs and sobs.

"Don't worry, Gloria, we won't give up," I say.

"No, of course we won't," shouts Dylan.

Eventually we manage to pull the plastic thing forwards, but we can't quite get it over poor Gloria's head to free her. It's very bendy, but also really strong. It stays stuck upright on top of her head, like a weird hat. Her eyes are red from all that crying, and the feathers on her neck are ruffled and spotted with blood.

"It's terrible – so many bits of plastic like this are floating in the sea," says Dylan.

"Yes, but what can we do about it?" Elliott asks.

"Let's start by telling all the other gulls what's happened to Gloria," I say.

"That's a great idea," replies Elliott. "This is important. If there's so much plastic out there, any of us could be the next victim – one of the seagull babies, or even little Amber here."

Amber's eyes glaze over, and her feathers turn a shade whiter. "Even me!" she gulps.

"We're all in this together," says Dylan. "Gloria, the Grabbos will do their best!"

"I'm really grateful," says Gloria, "especially to you, Poppy. You'll always be my friend."

I feel a warm glow.

"Group hug!" shrieks Amber, and she hurls herself at the rest of us with her wings outstretched.

I put my wings out too, and we all make a circle round Gloria. We solemnly bow our heads, wings touching.

Chapter Three

"We'll invite every gull we see to come and meet us on the beach," I say. "Elliott, you tell everyone over at the marina. We'll round up all the others. Do you feel well enough to join in, Gloria? We really need you there."

"I'll be OK. Of course I'll come," she replies bravely.

Hundreds of gulls turn up, which is great. Some of them are here because they're our friends, some want to find out what's going on, and the rest have just followed the others. We face the crowd, with Gloria at the front.

Amber kindly puts one wing on Gloria's back to comfort her.

"Just look what's happened to me," starts Gloria, but her voice is weak and she can't be heard above all the squawking from the crowd.

"Please listen!" I shout, but no one does. Then Elliott and Dylan do something that makes everyone stop and stare – they jump in front of Gloria and start to dance. They're doing the seagull shake, and all the young gulls are very keen to learn it. There's a lot of tail-wagging and wiggling from side to side, with wings clapping to the beat. When they finish, they stand still and point at Gloria.

"This is Gloria, and there's something very important we must tell you about what's happened to her," Elliott announces.

"And if you listen carefully, we'll teach you all how to do the seagull shake," adds Dylan.

I tell Gloria's story, and the gulls listen in silence. Then a voice calls out: "I've seen all the plastic on the beach and in the water. But I didn't think it could be so dangerous."

"Maybe you were just unlucky, Gloria," says

another. "What do you expect us to do? I don't think it's really a problem."

"Of course it's a problem!" shouts a large gull from the back. "What's happened to Gloria could happen to any of us."

"Even me," says Amber quietly. She looks worried. I put my wings round her and give her a special hug to comfort her.

"There seems to be as much plastic in the sea as fish," says Dylan gravely. "I guess the humans don't know what to do with it, so they dump it in the ocean."

Out of the corner of my eye I can see a human dropping a plastic sandwich box onto the sand. The wind blows it along the beach, where it lands next to more pieces of litter.

Another human comes along and picks it up. He has a stick with a sort of beak on the end, which he's using to grab litter and put it in a sack. It looks like some humans do care about what happens to their rubbish.

The other gulls are quietly thinking about what Dylan has said. "But what can we do?" asks one of them. "We're just birds. We can't change things by ourselves."

Amber still looks upset. I look at Gloria, and suddenly I feel brave. I step forward. "We can't give up!" I squawk. "We're not JUST birds, we're CLEVER birds. We must all put our beaks together and think of a plan."

"Where does the plastic come from," asks one gull, "and why do the humans throw it away?"

"They must have too much of it," I say.

"Maybe there are plastic families?" wonders Amber. "The big bits of plastic have babies, and the little pieces we see lying around are those babies."

"And the plastic families live in big buildings," says Dylan, liking Amber's idea.

"No, those buildings are factories," Gloria tells us. "I don't think the plastic can have babies. It's the humans that make plastic, inside the factories."

"Well, we'll have to think of a way to stop these factories making so much of it," I say. "We have strong beaks. We could attack the factories and peck at them."

The gulls start to mutter. Some of them flap their wings and shake their heads. "You couldn't even peck that thing off Gloria's head, so how can we damage a factory?" shouts a voice from the crowd.

I feel myself turn pink with embarrassment.

"I know! We have a much better weapon!" says Dylan enthusiastically. "We gulls can produce loads of poo – and we can fly. So why don't we all fly over these factories and bomb them with as much poo as possible? Our poo must be runny, and it must SMELL!"

"Ha ha ha!" The crowd erupts with laughter. Everyone loves his idea. "Yes!" "Hooray!" "Well done, Dylan, that's a brilliant plan!"

Dylan is so excited he almost falls over into the crowd, and has to be pulled back by Elliott.

"There are thousands of us gulls here, where we live," I say, "but there are loads more farther away who could come and help us. Then we could split into groups, and each group could bomb one factory with poo."

All the gulls cheer. I stretch my wings as high as I can.

"Gullpower for ever!" I squawk at the top of my voice, and everyone joins in.

Chapter Four

"It's time we started training," I say. The four of us are sitting with Gloria on the rocks by the lighthouse. "First, let's try out different foods so we can work out the perfect diet for the best poo."

They all agree.

"Why don't you rest here until you feel a bit stronger?" I ask Gloria.

"Yes, Poppy, I will. My neck's still sore," she says sadly.

"We'll have to eat as much of one thing as we can, and remember how effective it is," suggests Dylan. "I think I'll start with ice cream."

So we fly off towards the beach, leaving Gloria resting in the sunshine.

Then I see Red Top. She looks happier now, and she's scooting along the seafront. She's going very fast. But then …

"Oh no! She's fallen over!" I squawk, and we all dive down to check on her. But she's OK – she gets up and smiles.

"Good job I was wearing my helmet, Mummy," she says.

"Yes Darling," answers her mum. "You'd have really hurt yourself if you hadn't had it on."

I'm surprised to hear that. "Red Top's helmet looks as if it's made of plastic," I say to the others, "so some plastic must be useful. Humans can use it to protect themselves."

"Yes, but there's no excuse for throwing it into the sea when they've finished with it," says Dylan, frowning.

We head on down to the beach café.

"OK – you try ice cream, Dylan, and I'll give crisps and chocolate a go," shouts Elliott as we land near the café. We all start to tuck in.

"Try the chilli-flavoured crisps – they're lovely ," I suggest.

"I've had three packets already," says Amber, scooping several chocolate buttons and a cheese straw into her beak.

"I'm not going to try chips, because a tummy full of chips will make it hard to fly," says Dylan, looking sad.

"Ughmm! Ugghh!"

"What's that funny noise?" I ask. Elliott is flapping about and trying to talk, but his beak is stuck firmly shut by something brown and gooey.

"Oh no! He's plunged his beak into that tin of syrup, and now he can't speak!" I say. "Quick, we need to wash it off with seawater."

"Poor Elliott," says Amber kindly, as she takes his wing and leads him down the beach. Dylan and I follow, and between us we get rid of all the syrup.

"I don't think I'll try that again!" mumbles Elliott.

"Let's visit our favourite restaurant," says Dylan. "Who's coming with me?" But then we see some crows we know rushing to pick up a pink plastic glove. Colin gets there first, but two of the others tease and bully him so much that he drops it. Charley moves in and scolds them.

"Give that back – Colin had it first!" she caws.

"Well done Charley," says Dylan. "It's good to see her sticking up for Colin."

Amber is still fussing over Elliott, so Dylan and I head off to the restaurant to see what we can scavenge. We start stuffing ourselves as soon as we arrive.

"Delicious!" says Dylan with a grin. "I can feel this mixture of ants and cabbage starting to have an effect already!"

We both fly off to eject the food that's quickly working its way through our insides. We're giggling hysterically. In fact, we're laughing so much that we don't look where we're going – and suddenly we find ourselves in the middle of the group of crows.

"So what's making you two so happy?" snaps Charley, her wings on her hips. "Are you looking for plastic? That pink glove belongs to Colin."

We're surrounded – this is not good!

"No, we don't want your plastic," blurts out Dylan. "In fact, we're going to try and stop the humans throwing so much of it away."

"Stop them throwing plastic away? Are you crazy?" shouts Charley. She's spluttering so much I think she's going to explode. Even Colin, who is usually quiet and shy, is looking cross. My legs begin to shake.

Then we hear a familiar noise: "Brng brng!" It's the bell on Red Top's scooter. "Out of my way!" The birds scatter. My friend has come to our rescue. I'm so relieved and happy.

"Thank you, Red Top," I squawk as we fly to safety.

Gloria greets us when we get back. "I'm feeling a little stronger," she says in a feeble voice. The plastic thing is still stuck round her neck, and rubbing a sore patch. Dylan and I tell the others about our scary time with the crows.

"They'll try and stop us because they love the plastic so much," I say. "We need to explain to them how dangerous it can be. Then perhaps they'll decide to help us."

We can see a group of crows picking up some plastic wrappers. They take them to a large rock near the old ruined pier, where they stand and admire their shiny treasure. Then they cover it with pieces of tin foil, which sparkle in the sun.

"We could try bribing them with plastic," suggests Elliott. "If we give them some more of their precious treasure, they might listen to us."

"No," I say firmly. "They need to know that plastic can be harmful to them too. Crows do remember things. They'll remember if we're kind to them. So let's try and bribe them with food. They love their food."

"Like me!" grins Amber, licking her beak.

"Great idea," says Dylan. "We need to get our enemies on our side."

"So that's our plan for the crows," says Elliott. "Do you feel well enough to come and sample some more tasty snacks, Gloria?"

"OK, I'll do my best," she replies.

We all fly back to the café and gorge ourselves again.

"I'm enjoying this fruit cocktail with prawns and jam doughnut," says Gloria, who's managing to gulp down a few mouthfuls, even with the plastic round her head.

"My favourite is still crisps with jelly," says Amber. "Yum!"

After trying out lots of different sorts of food, we find that a mixture of rotten fish, seaweed and ice cream makes really good poo – very runny and very smelly!

We spend the rest of the day practising aerobatics. Soon we have it timed just right, and can shoot out squirts of revolting poo at top speed. What an amazing performance!

Chapter Five

Now that we Grabbos are expert dive-bombers, it's time to train the other gulls. They'll need to make their wing muscles stronger. And we must make sure they can all fire their poo accurately from different heights. We all head for the beach.

"Right," I call out, "who's ready for some flying practice?"

"We can already fly!" one answers back.

"I know," I say, "but we need to do some special training."

"I've flown a few marathons," says Elliott. "I can give you some tips. Let's start by flying out

23

to the windfarm. Copy what I do. Don't worry if you can't keep up to begin with – you'll get stronger if you keep practising."

First, we do ten laps of the windfarm, with Elliott taking the lead. Sometimes we flap our wings vigorously, and sometimes we glide if the wind is in the right direction. Then, we fly closer to the turbines. We duck and dive between the huge sails as they turn in the wind.

"I'll see you later," I squawk after a while. "There's a factory not too far from here, which could be our target factory. I'm off to check the best way to get there."

"Can I come with you, Poppy?" asks Amber. "We might be able to grab some food on the way."

I smile. Amber is always thinking of her stomach. "I can't believe you're so tiny when you eat so much!" I say. "Come on, let's go. We need to head back to shore."

On our way, I notice a small fishing boat bobbing about on the waves beneath us. There are two men on the boat.

"This is hungry work," one of them says. "Let's have our lunch now."

He takes a small parcel out of his bag and unwraps it. It's a delicious-looking sausage roll, and it seems to be inviting us to eat it. I swoop down and grab it from the man's hand. I give it to Amber.

"I hate those seagulls!" the man shouts.

"Here, have one of these," says his friend, offering him a handful of sardines.

I don't have to think twice – I lunge at this new prize and grab myself a yummy fish.

"Get out of here!" shout both men, and they start throwing things at me. A plastic bottle strikes me on the side of my head, and falls into the sea. My head stings, and I drop my mouthful in surprise. The partly chewed sardine lands on the man's bald head. He stands there shouting at me, waving his fists wildly, as bits of sardine slither down the side of his face.

"Are you OK?" asks Amber. "You look even whiter than usual."

"I'm fine, thanks," I reply, even though my head is throbbing.

We fly on towards the beach. I can see lots of rubbish – plastic mesh, shiny yellow ducks, little white balls – all floating on the waves below us. It doesn't look like treasure to me, though that's what the crows think it is. I've seen how harmful it can be. A lump forms in my throat as I think of Gloria.

As soon as we reach the shore, we fly inland and over the fields. In one field there are two barns. They must be very old, and they look as if they're about to fall down.

Then we spot some of the crows in a field of corn. Cassius is taunting a scarecrow in the middle of the field, to show the others how brave he is. Suddenly, he jumps up and grabs the scarecrow's hat. He tosses the hat across the field, and it lands on Charley.

"Help! I can't see where I'm going!" she caws. She flaps and flaps until the hat falls off. Then she stands still, wings on hips, with her head feathers all sticking out.

"Now you look just like the scarecrow!" says Cassius, and the other crows all laugh. Eventually, Charley sees how funny it is and starts laughing too.

"It might be fun to have the crows on our side," wonders Amber.

"Yes – we must try hard to get them to join us."

As we fly on, we can feel the wind getting colder and stronger.

"I think there's a storm coming," I say. "Let's go faster."

We're now over a town, and we can see a lot of buildings and roads jammed with traffic. The wind is getting even stronger, and it's so noisy I have to shout. "We're nearly there!" I squawk loudly to Amber. "Try and keep up with me – I don't want to lose you."

But then we're caught by an enormous gust of wind. Little Amber is being flung towards a huge building. It's the factory I thought we could attack. Her eyes are wide open in fright as the wind hurls her forwards and makes her do somersaults. Using all my strength, I fly after her and manage to push her away just in time to stop her crashing into one of the huge chimneys.

Phew! The storm passes, and we've come to no harm. Now that we've checked the route to the factory, we can start to fly home.

"We need to get back to our nests before it gets dark," I say.

"But my wings are really aching," moans Amber. "Can't we just stop for a bit?"

So we have a rest in the field with the scarecrow. I can see a scarf tied tightly round its neck. It reminds me of Gloria, with her head trapped in plastic. We're both feeling tired now. I puff out my feathers to make myself comfortable. Then we hear a loud noise – "CAW!" "CAW!" "CAW!"

About twenty angry crows have arrived, led by Cassius. Their wings and shoulders are hunched up, making them look like vultures. They form a circle around us so there's no way we can escape. It's beginning to get dark now, and I'm absolutely terrified. But I think about Gloria suffering – which makes me angry. And that gives me courage.

"Let us out!" I shriek in a loud but wobbly voice. "You're in our way. Why don't you all just BACK OFF and let us get on with our important mission!"

I almost faint after this outburst. What have I done? How could I have been so stupid? And to make things worse, I can see that Amber is standing with one foot on a shiny plastic bag! This makes the crows even angrier. They glare at me, and I can see the whites of their eyes. They point their beaks menacingly at me.

"YOU are just a scrawny little gull," shouts Cassius, "and now you've dared to shout at ME!" He struts towards me until his great big beak is almost touching mine. He stares right into my eyes. Then he laughs so loudly I can feel his spit landing on my face.

"But I am rather impressed," he says. "I admire someone with guts."

I shake my head to try and get rid of his awful spit, and I start to squawk and tremble.

"Keep your feathers on!" he bellows. "Now, what's this important mission you were talking about?"

By now, I'm shaking so much I can hardly stand. Amber is so frightened she can barely move, and her beak is half-open. But somehow I pull myself together, and I tell Cassius what happened to Gloria and how we fear for all the chicks, and also that crows could be in danger too.

"Remember when you were playing with the scarecrow's hat?" I ask him. "What if that hat had got stuck on Charley's head, and she couldn't get it off? It wouldn't be funny then." I explain our plans for the mission. I put in a few extra details, thinking a bit of flattery might be a good idea.

"You crows are much faster and stronger than us," I say as nicely as I can. "If you join us, we can succeed! We know you love shiny plastic. The trouble is, it can be very harmful if it's left lying around."

I nod to Amber, who's looking a bit more relaxed now. Then I turn round three times, look up at the sky and let out one great big

"SQUAAAAAWK!"

At this signal, Amber and I begin to jump up and down on the spot – and the crows can soon see why. Suddenly, the grass is covered with fresh, juicy, delicious earthworms that have popped up out of the ground.

"Help yourselves," I say to the crows, politely pointing at the worms with my wings. The crows tuck in greedily.

After they've all gorged themselves on the surprise feast, the crows are a lot more friendly. Cassius stands silently, his wings crossed in front of his big black belly. He gives me a look of respect, and I feel myself begin to blush. Then he speaks. "Come on guys," he says to the other crows. "The gulls need our help!"

Chapter Six

I round up all the gulls who want to help, and Cassius leads us to the old pier, where lots of crows are waiting for us. Now's our chance to tell them more about plastic pollution. It seems strange – we used to be enemies, but now I'm trying to get us to work together.

"We're here today to find a way to help the gulls," announces Cassius. "They've discovered something terrifying about the plastic we love to collect."

As soon as the crows see Gloria, there's a great commotion. Some of them jump up onto the railings, cawing at the tops of their voices. I can feel a lot of tension. The angriest crows start to make trouble by edging up against gulls and barging at them with their strong shoulders. The gulls don't like this, and start to peck back.

Charley tries to stop them, but she falls on top of one of the gulls and squashes him – which just makes things worse. Gloria looks really tired, so Amber holds her wing gently to comfort her. We all feel frightened.

Cassius takes control. "You all need to listen," he shouts as loudly as he can. "And stop hopping backwards and forwards on the railings while we're trying to speak!"

"Yes, it's very annoying," I say. But straight away I wish I hadn't, because Cassius gives me the scariest stare.

"I'm doing my best, Poppy," he snaps back. Then he glares menacingly at the rowdy crows.

"We all need to keep calm," I say.

"I've got an idea," squawks Dylan. "Come on, Elliott, let's dance!"

They both start dancing the seagull shake again, even more wildly than before. Charley joins in, and every time she spins round she slaps Cassius on the head with her tail feathers. Everyone – crows and gulls – starts to laugh, even Cassius. Charley looks embarrassed and hops away to the back of the crowd.

Eventually, everyone calms down.

"We gulls have a plan to drop loads of poo on plastics factories to put them out of action for a while," I tell the crowd. "And we need to let lots of other birds know about our mission. It's a huge challenge, but we've got to try and spread the news as far as we can. It will be like an enormous and very important game of Chinese whispers."

Cassius nods in agreement. "And we could get birds in other countries to help us too."

"Well, for that we'd need a translator," I add. "It could be Elliott. He's flown to other countries with his marathon club, and he can speak different Gull dialects. He can understand Gannet, Tern and Skimmer."

"My Skimmer's a bit rusty," says Elliott, glancing down at the ground and shuffling his feet. "But I think I could learn to speak Crow languages too."

"Excellent!" says Cassius, and slaps Elliott firmly on the back, almost knocking him over.

"And we need to start practising," I say.

Some birds in the crowd start to nod in agreement, but others don't seem convinced.

"Practise? Surely, all we need to be able to do is fly and poo at the same time?" says one crow.

"I've got another idea!" yells Charley. "We crows have strong beaks and we can pick up quite large, heavy things. You gulls are experts at pooing, but we could do even more damage by dropping stones on the factories."

She seems really pleased with herself. She smooths down her head feathers with one wing, and poses proudly. I think she's being a bit boastful, but the others love her idea.

"That's brilliant!" "Well done!" "Wow, that's perfect!" Everyone calls out at once.

Then Cassius speaks up: "All those in favour of Charley's proposal, let's hear you."

"SQUAWK!" "CAW!" "AARK!" – the noise is deafening.

So it's agreed that the crows will drop their ammunition on the factories at the same time as the gulls drop their poo.

"We need a name for this mission," I say. "Any ideas?"

"How about P-Day?" suggests Dylan, which makes all the birds laugh loudly.

"P-Day it is!" I cry. "Now let's start flying off to other countries. Are you ready, Elliott?"

"I was born ready!" replies Elliott. "If we can get as far as Egypt, my friend Ra should be able to help."

"Take Charley with you," says Cassius. "She could fly on to India. She knows some crows who live there and she could be our agent in Asia."

"Just what I was thinking!" caws Charley.

"I'm coming too!" I squawk.

"We Grabbos are in this together!" shouts Dylan.

"If you three go with Charley, I'll stay here and take care of Gloria," says Amber. "She still doesn't look very well."

The crowd murmurs in agreement.

"That's kind," I say. "We'll be back as soon as we can."

I'm so excited. How many other birds around the world can we get to join our mission? Maybe a million – or even more?

Chapter Seven

We set off straight away – three gulls and one crow, keeping each other company on the long flight.

Elliott and Dylan are busy teaching Charley a song to sing to the seagull shake. Charley makes loud rasping noises when she sings. Elliott tries to mimic her, which makes us laugh.

We've crossed the sea and we're now flying over land. The fields below us are making green and yellow patterns as far as I can see. Then we spot some crows coming towards us.

"Why are you flying with those gulls?" one of the crows asks Charley. "Why don't you join us?"

Charley explains about plastic pollution and our plan to strike the factories. The crows listen carefully.

"But how would we recognise the factories?" asks another crow.

"There's a funny smell and your eyes sting. Sometimes there's smoke as well, and it makes you cough when you fly over them," says Elliott. "I've seen them when I've been flying marathons."

"Oh yes, I think I know where one of those is," replies the first crow.

"Anyone who sees a factory should remember where it is," I say. "And don't forget to mention that crows and gulls are working together on this!"

"OK, we'll see what we can do," say the crows, and off they go.

"That was a good start," says Charley. "Let's hope all the other birds we meet will want to help too."

We flap our wings as hard as we can and set off on the rest of our journey to spread the message all around the world.

At last we reach the coast. I'm enjoying flying over the sea again. Now it's starting to get really hot, and I can feel the sun burning the feathers on my head. Eventually we reach a vast expanse of dry land.

"Welcome to Africa," says Elliott.

"This is where we part company," says Charley.

"Good luck!" we call out, and we high-five with the tips of our wings.

"I'm going to hitch as many lifts as I can," she shouts as she flies off.

She's boasting again, I think to myself, but the boys are impressed.

"What a brilliant idea!" says Elliott. "Look, there are some trucks going in our direction. Let's ride on them and see how far we can get. We need to give our wings a rest."

He is fearless. He swoops down and grabs hold of a windscreen wiper on the first truck. Dylan and I do the same, landing on the second truck. The drivers turn on the wipers to try and shake us off.

"Yee-ha! This is fun!" shouts Dylan, as the wipers go faster and faster. Then water squirts up at us from holes by the windscreen. But the drivers can't make us let go, and both trucks carry on with their uninvited passengers.

After a while, we decide it's time to give our beaks and claws a rest and start flying again. We flap our wings to say goodbye.

"I wonder how Charley's getting on," I say. "I hope she's met some helpful crows."

"Me too," says Dylan. "I'm getting tired. We're not used to flying marathons like you, Elliott."

"You two rest, and I'll fly on a bit further. I'll come back for you soon," promises Elliott.

He flies off. I can feel the hot African sun on my back. I'm beginning to feel homesick. Dylan starts messing about to cheer me up.

"There aren't any ice creams here for us to grab," he says. "Let's have a game of chase, or are you too tired?"

I'm always up for a game of chase, so I quickly lunge towards him before he has a chance to get away.

"Hey, that's not fair! You need to give me a start." As he's talking, he turns round to face me – but he doesn't look where he's going.

"Ouch! Ooh! Aaah! I've hurt my foot. Help!" he shouts.

I rush to his side. He's standing on something shiny, pointy and hard.

"It's digging into my foot and I can't get it out!" he squawks.

"Let me have a go," I say. I tug at the object with my beak, but it won't budge. There's a large twig on the ground nearby, so I grab it and start to prise the object off Dylan's foot.

"Ouch! Be careful, Poppy!"

"Hold tight! One more go and that should do it," I say.

I'm using all my energy, and my neck and beak are aching badly. I give one final heave, and Dylan's foot is free at last. He limps away, his feathers all fluffed up.

Suddenly, there's a loud rumbling noise in the distance. Something is heading towards us – but what is it? There's a beautiful tree not far away, with an enormous trunk and long branches spreading out. It looks like a huge open umbrella.

"We must fly up to one of those branches," I say. "I can hear strange noises and I'm frightened."

The rumbling sound is getting louder and louder. I can feel the ground wobbling beneath my feet. We stare at each other, beaks wide open.

"Quick!" I squawk. We fly up and land on a branch. And we're just in time – a herd of graceful brown and white animals is thundering towards us. Some of them have long, curved horns. Right behind them, darting to the right and then to the left, teasing them, is a large spotted cat. It runs so fast that the animals scatter everywhere as they try to escape. The cat continues to chase them, until I can hardly see them because of all the dust flying up from their hooves. They look very afraid – and so are we!

"And we used to worry about crows!" says Dylan, as the animals vanish into the distance. "It's lucky that big cat didn't see us."

"My foot still hurts," he whimpers after a while.

"I'll spit on it to see if that soothes the pain," I say.

"Thank you Poppy," he gasps.

As I bend down, I hear his tummy rumble.

"Let's see if we can find something to eat," I suggest.

We fly down to the ground. Dylan cries out in pain as he lands. He manages a hop, skip and jump, bending over with his bottom sticking up.

Then I notice Elliott flying towards us. "Dylan's been hurt!" I blurt out.

"Oh no! What's happened?" he asks.

"I trod on something very sharp," says Dylan. "And guess what it was made of?"

"Plastic," we both reply in disgust.

"Yes. But the good news is that my injured foot won't stop me flying. And I can still poo!"

We all laugh out loud.

Chapter Eight

We fly on towards Egypt. I'm worried about Dylan's injury, but he doesn't want to slow us down. "I'm fine!" he shouts. And to prove it, he dives down to scavenge some tasty insects and rotten fruit. "Delicious!"

The gulls we meet on our way are fascinated by our story. And we talk to a couple of crows who are impressed with Elliott's communication skills.

"They say they have relatives in Sri Lanka and Bangladesh," he tells us. "They're sure they can all help to spread the message – maybe even to India. There are millions of crows there."

We give the crows a firm wingshake before we leave them.

"Maybe they'll bump into Charley," I say.

When we get to Egypt, we meet up with Elliott's friend Ra. They both touch the tips of their wings affectionately and nod their heads respectfully. At first we don't get a chance to talk about the mission. All Ra wants to hear about is life in England.

"Great to see you," says Ra. "How is Amber? Do you all still play Grab the Ice Cream?"

"We'll catch up later," replies Elliott, "but first we need to tell you about our mission."

Ra listens to us, but he seems doubtful. "I'm not sure about getting the crows to join in," he says, a worried look on his face.

"Don't worry about them," I say. "They're on our side – we used worms to tempt them! And they're going to drop stones on the factories when we drop our poo."

"Some of my friends have joined a marathon flying club here in Egypt," says Ra. "If they fly off to spread the word, we could get the news as far as South Africa. Then we'll need to work out how to tell our cousins in America."

Dylan's been very quiet while we've been talking. His eyes are closed and he's huddled up in a ball.

"Dylan!" I cry. "You're not fine, are you?"

"No, my foot really hurts," he gasps.

"That looks very painful," says Ra. "You need some medicine. I'll find you some bitter melon leaves – they should do the trick." He rushes off.

"I do hope they'll make you better," I say.

Ra soon comes back with some leaves in his beak, and gently wraps them round Dylan's injured foot. The leaves work their magic, and the pain begins to go away.

As soon as Dylan is better, we three Grabbos start to fly back home. On the way, we meet many birds who've heard about the mission and are very excited.

"I've just come back from Nigeria," says one. "Some of the gulls there have hitched a ride on

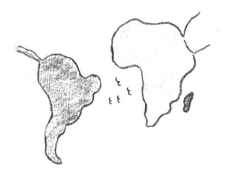

a ship sailing to Rio de Janeiro. They'll spread the message across South America."

"That's right," says another. "And I've heard that some crows in South Africa are going to hop onto a ship that's going to Sydney, so the message can get to Australia."

"This is all happening much faster than I would ever have guessed," I say, amazed that our plan is working so well. "I reckon we'll have millions of gulls and crows ready for action on P-Day."

Chapter Nine

We're home, and Charley's back from India. The first thing I do is rush off to check on Gloria. She still has that horrible plastic thing round her head, but she does seem a bit better. I give her a hug, and she chokes back a tear.

"Well done, Amber," I say. "You've done a great job looking after Gloria."

"We went to the farm where she grew up," replies Amber.

"Amber helped me make a comfortable bed on the roof of the old barn where I was born," says Gloria. "I rested a bit, while she went off to rehearse with the other gulls. They've worked out the most effective food to stuff themselves with on the days before the mission – and how much they can cram into their stomachs."

"While you've been away, I've worked my way through a menu of mice, insects, seeds, fruit, fish, crabs and worms," says Amber. She taps her belly and emits an enormous belch.

I go down to the beach to find Cassius.

"The crows have been busy collecting ammunition," he tells me. "We can't wait to start. We've been training hard for the long flight. And we can dive-bomb at 60 miles per hour and still hit our targets."

"Impressive!" says Dylan.

"There's your friend," says Elliott, pointing down the beach.

I recognise her red top. Maybe she's got a treat for me! We fly closer.

"Look at all this rubbish on the beach, Mummy!" I hear Red Top say.

Then she and her family bend down and start to pick up pieces of litter.

"It doesn't look nice, and I'm worried the birds might get ill if they mistake it for food and eat it," says her mum.

They collect the rubbish around them and put it in Red Top's bucket. I'm quite confused.

"So that plastic bucket is useful," I say to the others.

"Yes, it's just the stuff humans throw away that we need to worry about," adds Elliott.

Charley comes to join us. "When I was in India, I told the crows I met to search for some of the plastics factories in Asia," she says, "and now the group leaders know which ones they're going to attack."

"Good work, Charley!" I say. Then she hugs me so hard that she sweeps my feet off the ground and my beak gets wedged under her chin! When she puts me down, I have to get my breath back before I can speak.

"Remember – it's very important not to harm any humans, just their factories," I say.

"And if they can see how angry we are, it might make them stop and think." All the birds nod their beaks in agreement.

"We've had spies at every factory here, and they know which chimneys and skylights to aim for. After we hit those, we must attack windows and doorways, and block them all with stones and masses of poo. Good luck, everyone. This is a job worth doing!"

Chapter Ten

It's almost P-Day! I meet Cassius to make our final plans.

"The crows have collected thousands of stones," he tells me proudly. "Come with me and I'll show you."

We fly to a nearby field, where there are two derelict barns. I remember seeing them when Amber and I flew to the factory. As soon as we get there, I sense that something is wrong – but I'm not sure what it is. I have a funny feeling in my stomach.

"This is where some of our guys have been

stashing ammunition," says Cassius, and he flies over to the door of the first barn. As I follow

him, I can see through the gap between the two barns. That's what I could sense!

"Look, Cassius!" I squawk. "Can you see those bulldozers? They look ready for action! The farmer must be getting ready to knock the barns down."

"This is really bad news," says Cassius. His head hangs low and his shoulders are hunched. "I've let you down, Poppy. We won't be able to use the stones if they're buried under rubble."

"We can't let anything go wrong now," I reply, trying to stay positive. "We have to fix this. Let's both go and get as much help as we can."

We rush off and come back with lots of other gulls and crows, all eager to try and save the barns. Colin, the crow with the unusual beak, stays at the back of the crowd, looking uncomfortable about joining in.

"Split yourselves into groups and attack these machines," I order. "Do whatever you can to stop them working."

Well, we all do our best. We dive, we peck and we claw at the bulldozers, but it's no use. We're helpless against these metal giants. We flop down onto the grass together, breathless and disappointed.

"Looks like P-Day will have to go ahead without our help," says Cassius sadly. "I'm sorry, Poppy."

My eyes fill with tears. It would have been so fantastic for us all to work together as a team. Then we hear the cry of a solitary gull circling overhead. As she comes closer, we recognise her.

"It's Gloria!" cries Amber. "This is part of the farm where she grew up."

Gloria lands beside us. She looks exhausted and her neck looks very sore where the plastic is still rubbing against her.

"I've been watching you all pecking at the bulldozers, but we need to try a different tactic," she says. "If we want to put them out of action, we must stop their engines working."

"How can we do that?" I ask.

"I've seen humans pouring liquid into tractors through a hole in the side. The liquid is petrol, and it's what makes the tractors and bulldozers work. We need to try and pollute the petrol."

"Are you sure?" asks Cassius.

"Yes," replies Gloria. "One day, the farmer was very cross because dirt had got into the petrol and stopped his tractor working."

Then she starts to cough and splutter. She's worn herself out flying here with that thing round her neck. She collapses at the side of the field. We Grabbos tiptoe quietly over to Gloria to comfort her. Amber lies down beside her and strokes her head with one wing.

"Poor Gloria should NOT be suffering like this!" I shout. "She's been so brave to fly all the way here." Now I'm even more determined not to give up. Some of Cassius's confidence must be rubbing off on me! "You heard what she said – let's find a way to open the petrol caps."

Every bird obeys at once. But though we try our hardest, we just can't move any of the caps. We all stand around feeling helpless. Morale is very low.

Then Colin steps forward. "Maybe I could have a go?" he asks quietly. "My beak has a hook on the end and it's very strong."

"Impressive!" says Dylan.

Colin starts to prise open the petrol caps. While he's busy doing that, we gulls fly off and collect as much rotten fish as we can hold in our beaks. As soon as we return, we begin to stuff the fish through the caps that are open.

Some of the crows are starting to look embarrassed. They move away from the others and try not to make eye contact with them. Colin works quickly and silently. He hooks the crooked end of his beak under the rim of each cap and pulls and tugs until it comes off. He has to work really hard, and we can see the muscles on his back ripple and stretch under his feathers. He starts to sweat. The crows who'd hopped away now come slowly back.

"Colin, I'm really sorry for teasing you about

your beak. I feel very ashamed," says one, before backing away with her head bowed low.

"Me too," says another. "I didn't mean it. I actually think your beak suits you – it makes your eyes look bigger!"

One by one they apologise. Then the first one says, "I only teased you because I heard other crows mocking you and I didn't want to feel left out. I'm so sorry for hurting your feelings."

Colin pauses for a moment to show that he's heard them, then goes straight back to hacking at the petrol caps.

"Poor thing, he's sweating," say the crows who'd teased him. "Let's cool him down." They jump into a nearby puddle and flap their wings as fast as they can, splashing so much water that Colin gets a refreshing cold shower. He gives a shy smile.

At last, all the petrol caps are off, and the bulldozers are full of rotten fish.

"I think you deserve a group hug," I say to Colin.

"Good idea!" caws Charley, and she rushes over to give him a pat on the back. Unfortunately she slips on a rotten fish that's dropped onto the grass. "Oops!" she cries, as she slides into Cassius.

Then the Grabbos, Charley and Cassius gather round Colin and give him a grateful hug. It's a huge relief that the barn problem is sorted.

All around the world, crows and gulls have started to move closer to their target factories. Some of the humans notice that there are fewer birds around than usual.

We Grabbos head back to the beach to start stuffing ourselves. We fly over the field where Cassius stole the scarecrow's hat. The floppy black hat is now dangling from the branch of a nearby tree. The scarecrow's head has bits of bright yellow straw sticking out. Red Top and her family are having a picnic in the same field.

"Where are the pretty birds, Daddy?" I hear her ask.

"I hope they're a long way away, Pickle," replies her dad. "I want us to have our picnic in peace."

"Well, I'm going to leave some crumbs for my special seagull," says Red Top.

I feel a warm glow in my heart. As we fly on, I see a group of farmers below us. They're talking to a TV crew and they're being filmed.

"We're very happy because there are no crows on our land," I hear one of the farmers say. "We're sure it's our scarecrows who have performed this miracle. And we've come up with a new dance to celebrate." He starts to jig about in front of the camera while throwing bits of straw up in the air. "Now we can grow our crops without them being pecked at by hungry birds."

Two other farmers join in the dance. They leap about so much that one man's cap flies off and lands on a goat in the next field. And the farmers' children are doing cartwheels and somersaults in the background, sending startled chickens running off in all directions.

The humans seem very happy that we've all started to move away. But of course, they have absolutely no idea what is going to happen next!

Chapter Eleven

P-Day is here! "SQUAWK!" "CAW!" "AARK!"
It's as if starting-pistols are going off all over the
world.

"Let's see how much damage we can do,"
calls out Elliott.

"Yes, and remember – we're doing this for
Gloria, and for any other creature that's been
harmed by plastic," I squawk.

"I'm missing Gloria," says Amber, sadly.

"Me too," says Dylan, "but she does need to
stay at home. She's not well enough to come on
the mission."

Hundreds of thousands of birds take off. The sky turns black, as if it's night-time, because there are so many of us in the air. We're all moving together as if we're performing an amazing dance routine. Then we split up and head for our factory targets.

"Hey, what's that? Watch out!" There are more aircraft in the sky than the last time I flew this way. We're flying into danger, so I need to come up with an idea – and I'll have to act fast. I can't believe I'm having to step up again! I flap my wings as fast as I can, until I'm right at the front of the flock.

"FOLLOW ME!" I order at the top of my voice. I veer to the right, then straighten up just

in time to avoid a plane. I feel very proud of myself, and as I glance back I'm almost certain I can see Cassius winking at me!

Our group arrives at its target factory. I can see the chimney that Amber almost collided with the last time we were here. The smell it's making gets to the back of my throat and my eyes start to sting. But then the fun begins.

"Take aim and fire!" I screech.

"I've been practising shooting sideways," shouts Dylan, "so I'm aiming for that open window."

"Great shot, Dylan!" say Amber and Elliott together, as Dylan's poo strikes home.

"This is for Gloria!" squawks Amber, as a large splat of poo lands on top of the chimney.

"And this one's for all the plastic in the ocean!" shouts Elliott, squirting poo all over a skylight.

Now it's my turn. "This is for all the plastic bags and bottles that humans don't need!"

We unleash all our anger on the concrete monster below.

"This is the most fun I've had in ages!" shouts Dylan, as he prepares for another onslaught of diarrhoea.

The crows have all been spot on with their bombing, like darts players aiming for the bullseye.

"We need to circle back to get more ammunition," says Cassius.

"Make sure you don't collide with any gulls flying towards you," I shriek, "and make sure you don't get hit by their poo!"

The sky begins to look like a giant chessboard, with the white gulls and black crows crisscrossing one another.

The effect of thousands of birds dropping stones and poo at the same time is incredible. The noise of all the stones landing on the factory is like fireworks going off on New Year's Eve. And all our seagull poo is making the most terrible stench.

I can see humans near the factory. Some have put up umbrellas to protect themselves, but many of them are running home to take cover. Ones who are feeling brave are taking videos of this amazing sight.

"Gloria told me about videos," says Elliott. "Humans can send them to each other, all over the world."

"Then they'll find out that this bombardment by us birds is happening on every continent!" I say with a grin.

One by one, all the windows and doors of the factory are struck by volleys of poo and stones falling from the sky. The result is spectacular. We've succeeded in putting our factory out of action. There are mountains of stones in front of every door and window, and the roof is covered in what looks like cake icing, but is actually huge amounts of poo. And if the mission is going to plan, the same thing is happening in many other countries.

"Amazing," I squawk.

"Let's hope what we've done will make the humans stop and think about all the plastic they produce and then throw away," I say.

"I'd feel much safer going for a swim if there wasn't so much plastic in the sea," says Amber.

"I've seen humans who care about pollution," I say. "The other day I saw Red Top and her family picking up rubbish on the beach."

"And we know some plastic is useful," adds Cassius, "so perhaps humans will think about making only as much as they really need."

"Right, time to fly home," I say, "and the others can tell us all about their P-Day."

Chapter Twelve

The long flight home feels very different. On the way out, I'd been nervous but also excited about our fantastic mission. Now that we're nearly home, I feel relieved. But my wings are aching badly. My whole body is complaining about all the work it's had to do.

We fly back across the fields. I spot the scarecrow in the field where Red Top left me some crumbs, but all I can think of is getting back as soon as possible. At last I can see the lighthouse, and I know I'm nearly home. I force myself to fly faster.

Down on the seafront I see Red Top's dad showing his friends videos of the mission and talking about what's just happened all over the world. It makes me proud that such a huge and daring plan has worked so well. But what next? Was P-Day enough to change how humans think?

"I wonder if the humans will know why we bombed the plastics factories?" says Elliott.

"I really hope so," I reply. "They must realise we're angry, and perhaps they'll think more about what the plastic is doing to us birds."

"If not, they'll have us to deal with again!" says Cassius.

"Yes," I say. "Who'd have thought that gulls and crows would join together as one army to fight the evil of plastic pollution!" Then I have an idea. "Maybe we could keep in touch and help each other whenever we need to? It would be sad to lose contact now."

"Happy to hang around with you gulls," he grins.

"Thank you for everything, Cassius," I say to him. "You've proved to be a true friend."

Cassius looks secretly amused. "Always at your service," he replies. "No one has ever called me friendly before!"

As we land, we're met by Colin.

"I had to come back early," he says quietly. "Carrying the stones was tricky with my hooked beak."

"That's all right, Colin," I reply. "You did your bit earlier with the bulldozers."

"I came to tell you about Gloria," he says. "At first I thought she'd been captured by humans."

"Oh no!" all the Grabbos cry out.

"But it's OK. Some humans did come and take Gloria away, and we followed them to see what they were going to do with her."

"Where is she now?" squawks Amber, sounding very worried.

"They've taken her to a building where humans are looking after lots of sick birds. It has large glass windows, so we can see inside. They've got that plastic thing off Gloria's head.

She looks quite comfy, and she does seem happier."

"That's wonderful news," I reply. "I can't wait to see her. I promise I'll visit her every day."

"Me too," agrees Amber.

After we've rested, we all gather together on the beach – thousands of weary but extremely excited gulls and crows. I fly to a nearby rock, where everyone can see me.

"WE'VE DONE IT!" I squawk at the top of my voice.

"Group hug!" shout Elliott, Dylan and Amber together. Then, gulls and crows all pile on top of each other in one enormous, noisy, feathery black and white heap of joyful celebration.

Acknowledgements

I could not have written this book without the love and support of my whole family — in particular my husband, John, who has been my editor and proofreader throughout.

I also owe a huge debt to Kate Lee of Cornerstones Literary Consultancy, who has played a major role in the book's development.

About the Author

Joan Woodruff has always enjoyed writing for fun. (She once had a lengthy correspondence with the cat next door.) As a child, she wrote sketches for her friends to perform. As an adult working on the children's ward at the Royal Marsden Hospital, she wrote and produced many annual staff pantomimes. This is her first book.

 Matador

For exclusive discounts on Matador titles,
sign up to our occasional newsletter at
troubador.co.uk/bookshop